This book
belongs to...

Jason Rakany

Age 9

The Kincaid's book of

Wizards Giants Trolls and magic

BRIMAX BOOKS

NILS IN THE FOREST
(A Danish story)

Nils had spent the morning gathering firewood in the forest. When his sack was full with dry twigs he sat down under a tree, and took out his dinner. He had just unwrapped his bread and was about to take a bite from his cheese when a tiny dwarf with a long yellow beard appeared from nowhere and stood in front of him.

"Spare a coin so that a hungry old man can buy food," said the dwarf, holding out his wrinkled hand.

"I'm sorry," said Nils, "I have no coins, but I will gladly share my bread and cheese with you." And without waiting for the dwarf to reply he gave him half of what he had.

The dwarf ate hungrily and didn't leave a crumb. When he had finished Nils handed him his flask. "Wash it down with some ale," he said.

The dwarf drank exactly half, no more and no less, and handed the flask back to Nils. Then, without warning, he clapped his hands and disappeared as suddenly as he had appeared.

"Well I never," said Nils, when he had got over his surprise. "And not even a thank you for eating half my dinner."

Nils was on his way home, with the sack of firewood over his shoulder, when the trees around him began to tremble, and the ground beneath his feet began to shake.

'What can be happening?' thought Nils, trembling more than a little himself. He wasn't long finding out. Suddenly, towering high above the trees, was a troll wife. Some trolls are small. Some are big. Some are very big. And some are VERY BIG INDEED. This troll wife was even bigger than that. She was simply ENORMOUS!

"What are you doing in MY forest?" she roared, in a voice as loud as thunder.

"G.g.gathering firewood . . ." shivered Nils.

"No one gathers firewood in MY forest!" roared the troll wife. "I shall eat YOU for my supper."

"Please . . . don't do that. I have a wife and seven children at home. How will they live without me to look after them?"

The troll wife was in a playful mood. "Run and hide," she said, "and I will come and look for you. The first time I find you I will let you go. The second time I find you I will also let you go. But the third time I find you I shall EAT YOU . . . now off with you . . . run and hide!"

Nils dashed here, there, and everywhere in a panic. How could he hide from a troll wife? It was impossible. He had almost given up hope of escaping alive when the dwarf with the long yellow beard re-appeared.

"Do not worry," said the dwarf. "I will hide you." And taking his axe he chopped a splinter from a tree trunk. "In you go," he said. He pushed Nils into the space left by the splinter, then put the splinter back on top of him.

"She will never find you in there," laughed the dwarf.

He laughed too soon. When the troll wife came looking for Nils she was carrying an axe.

"Where are you going?" asked the dwarf.

"To cut down a tree, of course," said the troll wife. And she cut down the very tree in which Nils was hiding.

"Found you!" she said as she pulled him out. "Run and hide again," she said as she put him on the ground.

"Come with me," whispered the dwarf. He led Nils out of the forest and to the side of a lake where there were thick reed beds. He tapped Nils on the shoulder and Nils shrank to the size of a pin. Then the dwarf took a reed, broke it in two, put Nils inside the hollow stem, put the two halves of reed together, and put the reed back into the reed bed.

"She will NEVER find you in there," laughed the dwarf.

"Where are you going?" he asked, as the troll wife came up behind him with a sharp knife.

"Where do you think? To cut reeds of course." And with one big swish, she had cut them all.

9

"Found you!" she laughed, as she shook the reeds and Nils tumbled to the ground. "Now run and hide once more. Next time I find you I shall put you in my cooking pot."

Nils was in despair.

"Worry not," said the dwarf. "We'll outwit her yet." He dipped his hand into the lake and caught a fish. He broke it in two and placed Nils inside it. Then he joined the two halves together and threw the fish back into the lake. It swam away with a quick wiggle of its tail, and with Nils safe inside.

When the troll wife came looking for Nils she was carrying a wash tub and a fishing net.

"Where are you going?" asked the dwarf.

"To catch a fish for my supper of course," she laughed.

She pushed the wash tub into the water and climbed into it herself. She paddled with her hands until she was in the middle of the lake, then she took her fishing net and dipped it into the smooth, calm water.

"I can see the VERY fish I am looking for," she called.

The dwarf, who was watching from the shore, bent close to the waters edge and began to blow. He blew and he blew and he BLEW. What a storm he blew up. The wind howled! The thunder roared! The smooth lake became a raging sea. The waves grew higher, and rougher and rougher. The wash tub pitched, and turned and tumbled.

"Mercy! Mercy!" screamed the troll wife, clinging desperately to the sides of the wash tub.

"If you have ever shown mercy, then mercy will be shown to you," said the dwarf. Instantly, the wash tub overturned and tipped the troll wife into the lake. She was so heavy she sank straight to the bottom and was never seen again.

As soon as the dwarf was sure she was gone for good he stopped blowing and the lake became as calm as a puddle. He caught the fish, broke it open, took Nils out and restored him to his proper size. Then he put the fish together again and threw it into the lake. It swam away with a merry swish of its tail and without a backward glance.

The dwarf took Nils to the cave where the troll wife had lived. It was full of gold.

"Take it," said the dwarf. "It is all yours."

"Thank you . . ." gasped Nils.

"And thank you for the dinner you so kindly shared with me," said the dwarf. And with that he clapped his hands and vanished.

Nils never saw the dwarf again, but there was never a day which passed when he did not think of him, and the strange adventures that followed his appearance.

THE MAGIC BOOK

James Julian Smith worked for a wizard. Not mixing spells of course, the wizard did that himself, but dusting test tubes and apparatus, sweeping the floor, sticking labels onto jars of frogs legs, sorting ladybird eggs, and looking after all the other mysterious and wonderful things that wizards use. His most important job was dusting the magic book in which the wizard wrote all his spells.

The book was bound in leather and was so important it was chained to a table, and the table itself was fixed to the floor. It was very thick, and smelled of long ago, and mystery. It was a smell to make any nose tingle with excitement. James Julian wanted to see inside the magic book more than anything else in the world. The wizard used it every day, but whenever James Julian tried to look over his shoulder the wizard would bang the book shut and wait for him to go away. Whenever he had finished working on a spell he would lock the clasp of the book and put the key in his pocket.

One day the wizard went out on a collecting errand. There was a special ingredient he wanted for a spell and only he knew where it could be found.

"Carry on dusting," said the wizard, popping his favorite frog into his pocket as he went out.

"Yes Your Wizardship!" said James Julian.

He decided to start by dusting the book. Flick went the duster, flick . . . flick . . . James Julian stroked the leather cover gently with his finger . . . and made a startling discovery.

The book was unlocked! The wizard had FORGOTTEN TO LOCK THE BOOK!

James Julian stood staring at the book for a whole minute before he dared to open it. He turned the pages very carefully. Each one was covered with spidery writing and strange marks and symbols. James Julian couldn't understand ANY of it.

If only HE could cast a spell. Just ONE spell. Just a LITTLE one. He moved his finger along one of the lines of writing and began to read strange words that sounded like gobble-de-gook. There was a swishshshsh! A rush of cold air! A swirl of hissing round his ears! James Julian slammed the book shut so fast he almost caught his nose in it. He wasn't fast enough. The magic words he had just read had summoned a demon.

"What task do you set me?" asked the demon, hissing like a volcano.

James Julian was trembling so much he couldn't think of anything to say at all.

"Set me a task or I will strangle you," said the demon as though it was something he did every day.

"W.w.w.water that!" gasped James Julian pointing to a flower-pot standing beside the desk.

"It shall be done!" said the demon and left the room. He returned carrying a large barrel full to the very brim with water.

"No . . NO . . . NOT THAT MUCH!" gasped James Julian, "YOU'LL MAKE EVERYTHING ELSE WET!"

But it would seem that the demon had suddenly gone deaf for he poured every drop of water in the barrel over the flower growing in the flowerpot. James Julian was right. It WAS too much. It DID make everything else wet. It washed the flower right out of the flowerpot.

But the demon had not
finished. He fetched another
barrel of water and emptied that
over the flowerpot too . . . and then
another . . . and another . . . and then
another. And all the time the
demon was pouring, James Julian
was shouting "STOP! STOP! Oh
please STOP!" His voice got
very hoarse.

Before long the water was
swishing round James Julian's
knees.

Soon it reached his waist.
Pieces of apparatus began to
bob about like ducks on a pond.

"The book! I must save the
book!" James Julian grabbed the
precious book from the desk and
held it as high above his head
as the chain would let him.
Still the demon kept filling,
and emptying, the barrel. The
water crept higher and higher.

"Go away . . . oh, please go
away . . ." James Julian's voice
was worn to a whisper.

The water was already lapping round his chin. Any more and it would be over his head. James Julian couldn't hold his breath for ever. What WAS going to happen to him?

But just when he thought he was going to drown, the wizard returned home. The wizard knew EXACTLY the right words to dismiss the demon, send the water rushing out of the door, and the apparatus whizzing back to the shelves.

"At least you managed to keep the book dry," said the wizard as he took the book from James Julian's upstretched arms, "and it looks as though your arms will ache for a week, so we'll say no more, but let this be a lesson to you. Do not meddle with things you do not understand."

"Oh, I'll never do it again," said James Julian. And he didn't, but that was because the wizard never left the magic book unlocked again, and he didn't get the chance.

POET, GOBLIN AND DONKEY

Once there was a poet who could make up songs that would entice the fish from the sea, the birds from the sky, and the worms from the ground. The words he sang were as magical as any spell.

One day, the Queen's daughter fell into a sulk. The Queen sent for the poet.

"Your Majesty," he said, bowing very low. "Can I be of service?"

"The Princess woke this morning with a pimple on the end of her nose," said the Queen. "The only thing I know of that will cure it is the magic . . ."

"Oh, how kind," interrupted the poet. "How kind to say the magic of my songs will charm away a pimple and restore the Princess to her former beauty . . ."

"Don't interrupt . . ." said the Queen. "That wasn't what I was going to say at all. The only thing that will cure it in time for the ball tonight, is the magic ointment owned by the Goblin of the Rock. I command you to go and get it."

"But the goblin hasn't been seen for at least a hundred years," said the poet. "He NEVER leaves the rock."

"Then try your magic songs on him . . ." said the Queen.

It was a royal command, so the poet had to go.

The goblin was curled into a
tight ball in the very heart of
the rock. He was deaf to the
world, or so everyone thought.

The poet knew it was going
to be difficult. He knew he
would have to sing as he had
never sung before. He sang
softly with strange mysterious
words, and at last there was a
faint stirring inside the rock.
Presently the top of the goblin's
bald little head began to show.
The poet could see his forehead
. . . then two slanting eyes . . . then
a long pointed nose . . . then thin
lips . . . and a round chin. Then
two knobbly shoulders appeared.

The poet was drawing the goblin from the rock as gently and
as surely as a maiden draws a fine thread from a bundle of flax.
Now the tops of the goblin's spindly arms were showing . . . now his
bony elbows . . . now the poet could see the hand holding the precious
bowl of ointment . . .

At that precise moment a donkey brayed, right beside the poet's elbow. "EEE! AAWWW!" The poet's song had charmed HIM out of his stable, across a field, over a stream, through a wood, over a hill . . .

"EEE! AWW!" he brayed again, as though to say, "I've come!"

The poet was startled out of his wits and fell over backwards. The goblin was so frightened he shot high into the air in a tangle of arms and legs and rock dust.

Before the poet could recover his senses enough to catch him the goblin had disappeared into a new hiding place carrying the precious ointment with him.

And that's how it was that a proud princess went to a ball hiding the pimple on the end of her nose behind a fan.

It all goes to show that a poet's spell can be broken as easily as any other spell and that sometimes a poet can be too clever.

THE GIANT AND THE COBBLER

Once there was a grumpy giant who didn't like anyone very much. But more than anyone else he disliked the people who lived in the town of Shrewsbury. One day, he made up his mind he would get rid of them all – ALL the men, ALL the women, ALL the children and ALL the babies.

Running close by the town of Shrewsbury there was a river.

"I'll dam the river," said the giant, "and flood the town. Then everyone who lives there will drown."

It is very easy indeed for someone as big as a giant to dam a river. All he has to do is lift a shovel full of earth – a giant shovel of course – and drop the earth in the right place.

The giant was really rather stupid. Instead of waiting till he got to Shrewsbury before filling his shovel with earth, which he could have done quite easily, he filled it with earth outside his own cave.

It was a hot day. And even giants get tired, especially when they are carrying a lot of crumbly earth they are trying hard not to spill. Somewhere, it must have been when he stubbed his toe on a boulder and almost dropped the earth on his own foot, he missed the way.

"I appear to be lost," he said, and sat down beside the road – still holding the shovel of earth – and waited for someone to come and tell him which direction to take.

Presently, a cobbler, who had been to Shrewsbury himself to collect all the boots and shoes that needed mending, came by.

"Hello there!" boomed a voice high above the cobbler's head. The cobbler thought at first a hill had spoken. "How far is it to Shrewsbury?"

The cobbler was surprised, but he wasn't one to frighten easily and he thought to himself, 'Ho, ho, what can a giant like THAT be doing with a shovel full of earth like THAT . . . he's up to no good.' Aloud he said, "Why do you want to know?"

"I'm going to dam the river and flood the town so that all the people who live there will drown," said the giant.

'Something must be done about this . . . and quickly,' thought the cobbler.

"Do you know how far it is to Shrewsbury?" he asked.

"I do not," said the giant, and because he was lazy as well as stupid, he added, "Not very far I hope."

"I've just come from there myself," said the cobbler, who was as quick-witted as the giant was stupid. "It's been a very tiring journey I must say." He opened his sack and tipped all the worn boots and shoes he had collected for mending onto the ground. "That's how many boots and shoes I've worn out since I left Shrewsbury," he said.

"Really?" said the giant, looking surprised.

"Yes, really," said the cobbler, his fingers crossed behind his back because he wasn't telling the truth.

"Then it must be a very long way indeed," said the giant.

"Oh, it is," said the cobbler with a tired sigh, although the town of Shrewsbury was just over the next hill and if the giant had listened carefully he could have heard the town hall clock striking the hour.

"I can't possibly carry a shovelful of earth THAT far," complained the giant.

"If I were you I'd leave it here and go home," said the cobbler putting the boots and shoes back into his sack.

"That's good advice," said the giant, and tipped the earth off his shovel. It fell with a roar, like a cloud burst of dark brown rain, and when the brown dust had cleared the cobbler was standing beside a new hill. The giant was scraping his boots with the shovel. There was enough earth sticking to them to make a small hill beside the big one.

The giant went home and I'm glad to say forgot about the people of Shrewsbury. The cobbler mended all the worn boots and shoes and returned them to their rightful owners.

The two hills the giant made are there to this day. And so is the town of Shrewsbury, thanks to the quick thinking of a quick-witted cobbler.

A POT OF GOLD

Patrick lived with his mother, and a cow and some hens, in a tiny cottage in the middle of Ireland. They were poor, but they were happy.

Every morning, as she blew on the peat fire to make it hot enough to cook their breakfast porridge, Patrick's mother would call, "Wake up, and get up, you lazy boy! You will never catch a leprechaun with your eyes closed."

Leprechauns are fairy shoemakers. They live in holes in the ground and between the roots of trees. They are said to be very rich, and wherever there is a leprechaun there is sure to be a pot of gold hidden somewhere close by.

There were leprechauns living near the cottage where Patrick lived with his mother. The wind had only to stop blowing for an instant and Patrick's keen ears could hear the sound of their tiny hammers hammering against leather.

It was Patrick's dearest wish to find a pot of gold. But first he had to find a leprechaun to show him where there was one hidden.

"If you happen to see a leprechaun," said Patrick's mother, at least once every day, "Do not take your eyes off him for a moment. If you do he will disappear and then you will never find a pot of gold."

One day, when Patrick was returning home after another fruitless search, he heard the sound of tapping. He looked down, and there, in the long grass at his feet, was a leprechaun. He was so busy, hammering away at a pair of hob-nailed boots, he hadn't noticed Patrick.

Patrick moved very quickly.

"Got you!" he cried as he caught the leprechaun in his hand.

"Let me go! Let me go!" shouted the leprechaun, struggling to get free.

"Tell me where your gold is hidden first!"

"G.g.gold . . ." The leprechaun turned very pale.

"Yes . . . tell me . . . or I will not let you go . . . not EVER!"

"Quick! Look behind you! There's a cow in the corn!" cried the leprechaun.

Just in time, Patrick remembered NOT to look.

"Ha . . . ha . . . you don't catch me that way. I won't take my eyes off you. Now where is your pot of gold?"

"I haven't got a pot of gold . . ." cried the leprechaun. "Quick! Look behind you! Your house is burning!"

Patrick almost did look THAT time.

"You're holding me too tight," squealed the leprechaun. "You're squeezing the breath out of me!"

"It's no good trying to trick me," said Patrick. "I'm not letting you go until you tell me where your gold is hidden."

"I'll show you where it is," said the leprechaun.

Patrick took off his suspenders, tied them round the leprechaun's waist and put him on the ground.

"NOW you can show me," said Patrick, without letting go of the suspenders. The leprechaun led him to a field of thistles.

"It's under THAT thistle," said the leprechaun, pointing to an extra prickly one "You'll need a shovel to dig it up. You had better go home and get one."

Patrick thought quickly. How could he mark the thistle so that when he returned he would know which one it was.

"I'll put my garter round it," he said, and taking off one of the garters that held up his woollen socks, he placed it over the prickly thistle.

"NOW I'll go home and get the shovel," he said, "and to make sure you don't play any tricks on me I'll put you in my pocket."

Patrick ran home, got a shovel and ran all the way back. But when he reached the field, instead of digging, he sat down and howled. He cried and he sobbed. He held his head in his hands. Tears as big as raindrops rolled down his cheeks. Someone – I wonder who – had put a scarlet garter round every thistle in that field. There wasn't ONE thistle that did not have a scarlet garter for a belt. The leprechaun had tricked him after all. His mother had told him not to take his eyes off the leprechaun, hadn't she, and when Patrick put the leprechaun in his pocket that is exactly what he had done. He never saw another leprechaun and so he never found a pot of gold. His mother said, it was entirely his own fault.

THE CRYSTAL BALL

Once there was an enchantress who had three sons. She did not trust them for she was afraid they would steal her magic powers if they had the chance. She changed the eldest into an eagle and sent him to live in the rocky mountains. His brothers often saw him soaring amongst the clouds. She changed the second into a whale. He was condemned to live in the sea.

When Richard, the youngest of her sons, saw what she had done to his brothers he ran away before she could cast a spell on him.

He had many adventures, and then one day he heard about a king's daughter who was imprisoned in the Castle of the Golden Sun. Several brave men had tried to rescue her but they had all perished. Richard was brave, even though he had run away from his mother's magic, and he decided he would try to rescue the princess himself.

But first he had to find the Castle of the Golden Sun.

On his way through a forest he happened, quite by chance, to see two giants. They were quarreling. When giants quarrel it is very hard NOT to notice them. The earth shakes, the trees shiver, even the sky trembles. One of them saw Richard.

"Hey there!" he called. "I've heard small men are more clever than giants. YOU settle this argument for us!"

"If I can," called Richard. "What's the problem?"

"Which of us shall have the wishing cap?" asked the giant.

"Give it to me," said Richard. "I will walk a short distance. When I call, whoever reaches me first shall have it."

It seemed a reasonable answer so the two giants agreed. That way at least one of them would have the cap. If they carried on quarrelling the cap would be torn in two and then it would be no good to anyone.

Richard put the cap on his own head and began to walk, but he was so busy thinking his own thoughts he forgot to call out to the giants. "Ah," he sighed, "if only I could find the Castle of the Golden Sun." No sooner had he spoken than he was standing outside the castle gates. The wishing cap really was a proper wishing cap.

Richard found the king's daughter in a room deep in the heart of the castle. He couldn't help gasping when he saw her. She was SO wrinkled, and SO ugly, he wanted to turn his head away.

"This is not my real form," said the princess. "I have been bewitched. You may see how I really appear in the mirror, for a mirror cannot lie." The princess looked into her hand mirror so that Richard could see her reflection. She was very beautiful.

"How can the spell be broken?" asked Richard.

"He who holds the crystal ball in front of the Enchanter will destroy his power and I will become myself again," said the princess.

"Where can I find the crystal ball?" asked Richard.

"You must kill the wild bull that lives at the foot of the mountain. From it will spring a fiery bird which has in its body a red hot egg. The crystal ball lies in the yolk of the egg. You must make the bird drop the egg, but if it falls to the ground it will burn everything near it, and the egg and the crystal ball will melt. If that happens then the spell will never be broken." A tear fell onto her cheek.

"Do not cry," said Richard.

He found the bull exactly where the princess said he would. He killed the bull as the princess said he must and from its body rose the fiery bird. It rose into the sky and was about to disappear into the mountains when an eagle appeared. It was Richard's own brother in his enchanted form. As Richard watched, the eagle chased the fiery bird towards the sea. They were almost at the waters edge when the fiery bird dropped the egg.

It fell onto the roof of a fisherman's hut standing on the shore. Flames leapt from the thatch. Smoke billowed into the sky. Soon the egg, and the crystal ball it carried, would be melted in the heat

Just as Richard thought all was lost, a whale, Richard's second enchanted brother, swam close to the shore and caused a great wave to swell up over the beach. The rush of water swept right over the hut and put out the fire.

Richard searched in the wet
ashes until he found the egg.
The cold sea water had cooled it
so quickly the shell had cracked.
Richard peeled away the broken
pieces and found the crystal
ball inside, quite unharmed.

The Enchanter shuddered when he saw Richard had the crystal
ball.

"My power has gone," he said. "YOU are now the King of
the Castle of the Golden Sun." Then he left the castle never to
return.

Richard married the king's daughter and with the crystal
ball restored his two brothers to their rightful shape. They
all lived happily ever after, in the Castle of the Golden Sun.

MOLLY WHUPPIE

Once there was a poor woodcutter who found it impossible to feed all his children. One day he took the three youngest to the forest and left them there.

The children wandered, lost and hungry, until they came to a house. Molly Whuppie, who was the youngest, but by far the cleverest, knocked at the door.

"Please, will you give us something to eat?" she asked.

"Don't you know my husband is a giant and will eat YOU if he gets a chance?" said the woman who had opened the door.

"Please . . ." begged Molly Whuppie. "We are so hungry."

"Very well," said the giant's wife, and took them inside and gave them bread and milk.

When the giant came home for his supper he looked at the three strange children sitting at the table, and said, "Who are they?"

"Just three little children, very poor and thin," said his wife. "You eat your supper, I will look after them."

When night came, the giant's wife put Molly Whuppie and her
sisters to bed with her own three daughters to keep them safe.
After she had tucked them in the giant came and put golden chains
round the necks of his own daughters and chains of straw round
the necks of the three strangers so that he could tell them apart
in the dark.

As soon as the other children were asleep Molly Whuppie
moved the chains so that the chains of straw were round the necks
of the giant's own children.

In the middle of the night, when the owls were hooting and
the moon was hidden behind the clouds, the giant tiptoed into the
room and lifted the three children wearing chains of straw from
the bed and locked them in the cellar. "I'll soon fatten you up,
you'll make a tasty meal," he said.

"Quick . . . wake up!" whispered Molly Whuppie to her sisters.
She led them into the forest and they ran and ran, until they were
quite out of breath.

Next day they came to a house that stood beside a lake, and was surrounded by statues, and beautiful gardens. It was the house of a King. He invited them in and Molly Whuppie told him how they had tricked the giant.

"Ho, ho," laughed the King. "Well done! But I know of a better trick. If you go back to the giant's house and bring me the small sword which hangs beside his bed, your eldest sister shall marry my eldest son."

Molly Whuppie had to agree, that if she could do it, that would be a very good trick indeed. That night she went back to the giant's house and hid under his bed.

When the giant was snoring loud enough to make the rafters ring, Molly Whuppie took down the sword and crept towards the door. She was almost there when the sword rattled in its scabbard.

The giant woke with a roar!
"Steal my sword, would you!"
he shouted. He jumped from the
bed with a thud that shook the
whole house and ran after Molly
Whuppie. Molly was very nimble
and very quick, she dodged in and
out of the trees until they came
to the Bridge of One Hair. And
there the giant stopped chasing
her. The Bridge of One Hair,
crossed a very deep ravine. If
the giant had put one foot on it,
the bridge would have broken and
he would have been dashed to
pieces on the rocks below.
Molly Whuppie, who was as light
as a feather, skipped over the
bridge and escaped.

When her eldest sister had been married to the King's eldest son, the King said,

"That was a good trick you played on the giant, but I know of one better. Bring me the purse which lies under the giant's pillow and your second sister shall marry my second son."

That night, Molly Whuppie hid under the giant's bed again. When the giant was snoring fit to shake the roof from the house, she slipped her hand under his pillow and pulled out the purse. She had just reached the door when a coin dropped from the purse and rolled across the floor.

The giant woke with a roar! "Steal my purse, would you!" he shouted. He jumped from the bed with a thud that shook the house so hard a brick fell from the chimney. He chased after Molly Whuppie but she reached the Bridge of One Hair before he did and skipped over it to safety.

When Molly Whuppie's second sister had married the King's second son, the King said,

"That was a good trick you played, Molly Whuppie, but I know of one better. If you bring me the ring which the giant wears on his finger YOU shall marry my youngest son." Molly Whuppie thought THAT was a very good idea indeed, so that night she went back to the giant's house for the third time.

When the giant was snoring loud enough to shake down a whole forest, she slipped the ring from his finger. She was just putting it into her pocket when the giant opened one eye, very, very slowly, and looked at her.

"Steal my ring would you!" he whispered, though HIS whisper was as loud as a gale, and he caught hold of her.

"Let me go . . . let me go . . ." shouted Molly Whuppie.

The giant looked at her and said, "What would YOU do to ME, if I had tricked YOU as YOU have tricked ME?"

"I would put you in a sack with a dog and a cat, and a needle and a thread, and a pair of scissors. I would hang you up against the wall. Then I would go into the wood and cut the thickest stick I could find and then I would come home and beat you." said Molly Whuppie.

"Then that is EXACTLY what I shall do to you," laughed the giant.

And he did. When he had gone into the forest to look for the thickest stick he could find, Molly Whuppie stroked the cat and dog who were in the sack with her, and sang out, in a loud voice,

"Oh, if only everyone could see what I can see!"

"What can you see?" cried the giant's wife. "Whatever it is, let me see it too."

"If you really want to," said Molly Whuppie. She took the scissors, cut a hole in the bottom of the sack, and jumped out.

"You must get inside the sack if you want to see what I saw," said Molly Whuppie.

The giant's wife climbed into the sack and Molly Whuppie sewed her in.

It was dark inside the sack.
The giant's wife didn't like it,
and cried to be let out. But
Molly Whuppie had hidden herself
and would not reply.

When the giant returned home
with the thickest stick he could
find he began to beat the sack.

"Take that! . . . and that! . . . and
that!"

"Stop! Stop! It's ME!
It's ME!" shouted the giant's wife.

The cat began to yowl. The dog began to bark. There was
so much noise the giant didn't recognize her voice at first. By
the time he realised it was his wife in the sack and NOT Molly
Whuppie, Molly Whuppie was safely over the Bridge of One Hair.
He was VERY angry at being tricked again, but there was NOTHING
he could do about it.

Molly Whuppie married the King's youngest son, and everyone,
except maybe the giant, lived happily ever after.

PIXIE VISITORS

Pixies enjoy getting together and having fun. The trouble with pixies is, they always hold their parties at night when ordinary people are trying to sleep.

Once, there was a farmer and his wife. They had no one to help them on the farm and were always very tired at the end of the day. When the last chore was done they would put an extra log on the fire to keep it glowing through the night and go straight to bed.

One cold dark night, when there was frost on the hedgerow and icicles hanging from the roof, a pixie face peeped through the farmhouse window. The pixie took one look at the empty kitchen and the glowing fire and sent out a message. Before many minutes had passed the farmhouse kitchen was as crowded with pixies as a railway station is crowded with people in the rush hour.

It wouldn't have mattered if the pixies had had their fun quietly. But they didn't. Having fun to a pixie means squealing and shouting and screeching and singing. It means rattling and banging and slamming and clanking and popping. It means stamping and clapping. It means making a HULLABALOO!!! No one can sleep through it. Not even a tired farmer and his tired wife.

"Who is making all that noise?" cried the farmer's wife, sitting up in bed and pressing her hands to her ears.

"There are pixies playing in the kitchen," said the farmer who was on his hands and knees peeping through a hole in the floor.

"Then tell them to go and play somewhere else," grumbled his wife.

"I can't do that," said the farmer. And he was right! He couldn't! If he offended the pixies there was no telling what they might do. There are so many things on a farm that a pixie can make go wrong. They can curdle the milk and stop the hens laying for a start. If they are really annoyed they can make EVERYTHING go wrong.

"We'll just have to put up with the noise," sighed the farmer.

The farmhouse kitchen was warm and cosy and the pixies liked it so much they began to come EVERY night. The farmer and his wife hardly slept at all. They grew more and more tired. They just couldn't stop yawning during the day. When the farmer's wife fell asleep in the hen house and dropped all the eggs she had been collecting, the farmer decided the time had come to do something. But what? Offend the pixies and they were in trouble.

That night, when the pixies were making their usual hullabaloo, he peeped through the hole in the floor. The kitchen was like a fairground, with pixies swinging, and sliding and jumping, and dancing, and hopping, and skipping. They were rolling plates, banging spoons, rattling lids. They were twirling, whirling, climbing, leaping.

The farmer looked at their bright happy faces, and thought 'I can't spoil their fun.' But then he thought of all the eggs his wife had broken that morning and knew that something HAD to be done. If only he could think of a way to make the pixies leave of their own accord.

Right beneath him, sitting on a three-legged stool was the pixie fiddler. He was playing such a merry tune the farmer could feel his own feet twitching. Stop the fiddler and perhaps the party would stop too.

The farmer put his arm through the hole and carefully dropped a fork so that it went through the fiddler's coat tails and pinned him to the stool.

"Let go! Let go! LET GO AT ONCE!" The fiddler's shout was so loud the other pixies stopped in the middle of what they were doing to see what was happening.

"A giant! A GIANT!" they shrieked when they saw the arm coming through the hole in the ceiling. (To them it WAS a giant sized arm).

"A GIANT COME TO PUT US ALL IN A PIE!" they shrieked when they saw the fork.

They were so frightened they made themselves as small as flies and flew in a swarm through the keyhole. They were gone in a twinkling of an eye. The kitchen was empty. Well, almost.

The fiddler had made himself small too, but the fork was still pinning his coat tails to the stool, and try though he might he could NOT make the stool shrink. An ordinary sized stool will NOT go through a keyhole. It doesn't matter how hard it is pushed or pulled.

The farmer did not want the fiddler to hurt himself so he ran downstairs in his nightshirt and pulled the fork from his coat tails. The stool fell to the floor with a clatter and the fiddler and his fiddle shot through the keyhole like an arrow from a bow.

Whishshshshshshs . . . . he went, into the night.

The pixies never came back to the farmhouse. They found somewhere safer to hold their parties and the farmer and his wife were able to get to sleep at night.

LONG NOSE

Once there was a miller who had three sons, and a farmer who had a pretty daughter. One day, Roland, the eldest of the miller's three sons, said, "I am going to ask Margaret to marry me today."

In the lane leading to the farmhouse he met Old Molly. She was wrinkled and bent, and very ugly. Unkind people called her Mad Molly, and said she was a witch.

"Good day!" said Old Molly. "And where might you be going?"

Roland stuck his nose in the air and walked past her as though she wasn't there. It was a wonder he didn't fall over his own feet.

"No!" said Margaret, when Roland proposed. "I will NOT marry you."

A few days later, Robert, the second of the miller's sons said, "I am going to ask Margaret to marry ME today." He was quite sure he would succeed where his brother had failed.

Old Molly was gathering primroses in the lane leading to the farmhouse.

"Good day!" she said politely. "And where might you be going?"

Robert stuck HIS nose into the air and pretended to look at a bird which wasn't there.

"No! I will not marry YOU!" said Margaret when Robert asked her to marry him.

Robin was the third, and youngest, of the miller's three sons. He was kind and strong, but he had one fault. At least HE thought it was a fault. He had a very, long nose. A very, VERY long nose – the kind of nose that people laugh at. He wanted Margaret to marry HIM.

He met Old Molly by the farmhouse gate.

"Good day!" said Old Molly. "And where are you going?"

"On a hopeless errand," sighed Robin. "How can I expect Margaret to marry me when I have such a ridiculous nose. She has refused my two brothers, she is sure to refuse me."

"That's where you're wrong!" said Old Molly. "She shall marry you." She took a ring from one of her bony fingers and gave it to him. "Put that on and say 'Bless it'," she said.

Robin put the ring on his own finger.

"Go on, say what I told you to say," said Old Molly.

"Bless it," said Robin, and straight away his nose shrank half an inch. It really was quite surprising the way it happened, and how handsome it made him look.

"If Margaret refuses to marry you," said Old Molly, "Say 'Drat it' and then HER nose will grow half an inch. It will make her so ugly she will be glad to marry you."

"Thank you," said Robin. "I'll ask her right away."

When he got to the farmhouse Margaret was out.

"I'll wait," he said, and sat down. He began to day-dream and presently he closed his eyes.

Now, it so happened that there was another visitor at the farmhouse that day. He was an old miser who never spent a penny unless he had to. He was very rich, and Margaret's father, who thought being rich was important, wanted Margaret to marry him. The miser saw Robin sitting with his eyes closed and he saw the ring on Robin's finger.

'I'll take that, and give it to Margaret, then I will not have to spend money buying her a ring,' he thought. And very slyly, and very carefully, he took the ring from Robin's finger and slipped it onto his own for safe keeping.

Robin might have had his
eyes closed, but he wasn't asleep.
He knew exactly what the miser
was doing. As soon as the ring
was on the miser's finger he
whispered, "Drat it."

"OOOH," said the miser.
"Something has stung me!" He put
his hand up to feel his nose,
which was – you must have guessed –
half an inch longer than it had
been a moment before. "OOOOOH!
Something is making my nose swell!"

"Drat it!" whispered Robin
again. The miser's nose grew
another half inch. "Drat it!"
whispered Robin.

"What's happening?" shouted
the miser as his nose grew even
longer. "I must find a doctor at
once." So away he rushed, trying
to cover his nose with his hands.
It wasn't easy because the end kept
poking through his fingers.

When Margaret came home, she told Robin she had always loved him, even when his nose was long.

"Yes," she said, when Robin asked. "I WILL marry you."

The next time they saw the miser, his nose was still dangling like a parsnip.

"What AM I to do?" wailed the miser as he tried to prod his nose back into shape.

"Return my ring and give me a bag of gold, and I will cure you," said Robin.

"Anything, anything at all," promised the miser.

As soon as the ring was back on his own finger, Robin said, "Bless it!" He said it three times, and each time the miser's nose shrank half an inch. The miser was so relieved when it was back to its right size, he handed over the bag of gold without a murmur. There was enough gold in the bag for Robin and Margaret to set up house. Which goes to show, doesn't it, that it is always wise to be polite, especially if you meet a witch.

FRENCH ELF

French Elf was very fond of playing tricks. He never did anyone harm, but he sometimes made people feel very foolish.

One day he overheard two people talking.

"It is our wedding day a week from tomorrow," said Jeanne. "It is market day today. We must go into town and buy all the things we need to set up house."

"There will be a lot to carry," said Jules. "We must take the horse and cart."

French Elf chuckled to himself, and sat on a fence and teased some chickens to pass away the time while he waited for their return. With so many things to buy they were sure to forget something.

It was late afternoon before Jeanne and Jules returned. The cart was so loaded there was barely room for them on it.

French Elf leapt through the air, light as a goose feather, and sat on a chair leg behind them.

"Have we knives?" Jeanne was asking.

"Yes."

"Have we soap?"

"Yes."

"Then we have everything we need," said Jeanne with a happy sigh, and she snuggled up to Jules and began to dream about their wedding day.

The horse was trotting. The birds were singing. Jules was whistling. Jeanne was dreaming. And French Elf was waiting. He didn't have long to wait.

Suddenly, Jeanne sat up with such a start, Jules jerked on the horse's reins, and between them they almost upset the cart.

"Oh, no," wailed Jeanne.

A gleeful grin spread across French Elf's face. He rubbed his hands together in anticipation and his pointed ears twitched.

'Ho, ho,' he thought to himself, 'She's remembered something she has forgotten.'

"Whatever made you shout out like that?" asked Jules when they had quietened the horse and made sure nothing had fallen from the cart.

"I've forgotten to buy the thread the dressmaker needs to sew my wedding clothes," sighed Jeanne.

"Is THAT all! Surely you've got thread at home," said Jules.

"Only white . . . I need pink, and the palest of yellow, and apricot and delicate sky blue, and one with a touch of green in it. We shall have to go back to town to get some."

Jules sighed. It was a long way back to town, but he supposed he would have to go. He had the cart turned half way across the road when Jeanne cried out again.

"Look! Look!"

"What now?" grumbled Jules, who had quite enough to do trying to persuade the horse to take the right direction.

"Hey! Be careful!" he cried as Jeanne jumped from the cart.

"Look! A ball of thread!" And what a ball of thread it was! It had ALL the colors in it that she needed – pink, yellow, apricot, sky blue and delicate green.

"Oh, what a lucky thing I saw it," cried Jeanne.

"But how did it get there?" asked Jules.

"This isn't the time to be asking silly questions," said Jeanne, climbing back onto the cart.

Jules turned the cart homewards again and they continued on their way, with Jeanne carrying the precious ball of thread on her lap, and with French Elf doing somersaults on the chair leg behind them.

The dressmaker was very pleased when she saw the thread.

"It's absolutely perfect," she said. She was even more pleased with it as she sewed the wedding clothes. It was as smooth as silk, it didn't break, it didn't knot, and each color was exactly the right length.

The wedding day came, and everyone, and that included French Elf, gathered outside the church to see the new bride. How pretty she looked.

"What a beautiful dress!" everybody exclaimed.

And then it happened! Crick! Crack! The tiny colored bows decorating the skirt began to float to the ground.

"Ooh!" gasped Jeanne.

"What is happening?" gasped everyone else.

Crick! Crack! The muslin flowers decorating the bodice fell in a shower of petals.

Crick! Crack! The frill round the bottom of the skirt fell to the ground . . . then the skirt itself tumbled round Jeanne's ankles . . . the sleeves came apart and fell from her arms . . . the bodice fell into five different pieces.

Poor Jeanne was left standing in her petticoat, with her wedding dress in tatters around her. Someone ran from the crowd and put a cloak round her shoulders, and Jules took her home so that she could put on another dress.

"The thread I sewed with must have been rotten," said the dressmaker, who was blushing as scarlet as Jeanne herself. Oh, the shame of it all.

When everyone else had gone, she gathered the pieces together. She looked at them very carefully. She turned each piece over and over. She couldn't find one tiny piece of sewing thread anywhere. It had ALL disappeared.

"I should have known such perfect thread was too good to be true," she sighed.

The mystery was never explained, but then nobody had seen French Elf, had they?

THE BOASTFUL TAILOR

One day, a tailor who was always boasting about how clever he was, decided to go out and see something of the world. He walked a long way and at last came to a steep hill behind which he could see the tops of some trees, and a very tall tower. The tower was so tall it disappeared into a cloud.

"I'll go and see who lives there," said the tailor boldly. "I am afraid of nothing." He even boasted to himself.

He had only gone a few yards when something odd happened. The tower began to move. The tailor rubbed his eyes. Surely he must be imagining it? Towers don't move. But this one did. It stepped right over the hill and stood in front of the tailor. It wasn't a tower at all. It was a leg. A giant's leg. It was quickly followed by a second. And where there are two giant legs, there is bound to be a giant.

"WHAT DO YOU WANT?" bellowed the giant.

The tailor put his cupped hands to his mouth and called back, "I want to earn myself a crust of bread!"

"You may come and work for me," bellowed the giant. The tailor didn't think it was an offer he could very well refuse, since he was so small and the giant was so big.

"What wage will you give me?" he asked.

"I will give you three hundred and sixty five days every year, and an extra day every leap year," said the giant.

"That sounds fair," said the tailor, determined however, to make his escape as quickly as he could.

The first task the giant set him was to fetch water.

"Will one jugful be enough?" asked the tailor. "Or shall I bring the well? If the well isn't enough I will bring the spring too."

"No, no, the jug holds enough," said the giant. And he thought to himself, 'This is no ordinary man if he can fetch a well and a spring too. I must be careful what I say to him.'

The second task the giant set the tailor was to cut wood.

"Why not let me bring the whole forest and be done with it," said the tailor boastfully.

"No, no, there's no need to do that," growled the giant into his beard. "Fetch well and spring too . . . cut a whole forest! What sort of man is this?"

The third task the giant set the tailor was to shoot two wild pigs for their supper.

"I'll bring you a thousand," boasted the tailor.

"No, no, two will do," said the giant. And he muttered into his beard, "Fetch well and spring too . . . cut a whole forest . . . bring a thousand pigs. This man is dangerous. The sooner I am rid of him the better." He was so worried he lay awake all night trying to think of a way to get rid of the tailor.

The next morning the giant took the tailor to a marsh where willow trees grew. The giant picked up the tailor and sat him on one of the springy willow branches.

"I don't suppose even YOU can bend that branch to the ground," said the giant.

"Oh yes I can!" boasted the tailor. He took a deep breath and held it inside his chest, then he pushed at the branch. Slowly it began to bend.

"More . . . " said the giant.

The tailor pressed harder. The branch sank lower. The tailor's breath had disappeared. He needed to take a new one. He HAD to take a new one. But the instant he opened his mouth to breathe in, the springy willow branch hurled him into the air, like a catapult hurling a stone. Higher he went . . . higher and higher. He must have gone over the moon because he was never seen again, much to the giant's relief.

If the tailor hadn't been so boastful, he would probably be sitting at home now, telling his grandchildren about a giant he had once known.

THE TWO WIZARDS

Once there were three brothers. The two eldest spent all their spare time playing checkers, and the youngest spent all his time learning how to become a wizard. One day, Bertram, who already knew a thing or two about wizardry, said, to his brothers,

"I feel like having some fun. I will change myself into a horse, and you can take me into the city and sell me."

"What will happen when you are sold?" asked his brothers.

"It will be fun to find out," said Bertram.

Who should buy Bertram in his new shape as a white horse, but the King himself. He paid for him with twelve of the best elephants in the palace elephant stable.

"What are you going to do?" whispered Bertram's brothers as the King prepared to mount. "The King will behead you if he finds out you have tricked him."

"Don't worry about me," whispered Bertram. "Take the elephants and go home."

The white horse gave the King a splendid ride. No one else could keep up with him. When they arrived at the palace gate the King had to dismount to open the gate himself.

No sooner had he dismounted than the white horse bolted.

"Catch that horse! Catch that horse!" shouted the King. But by the time the grooms had mounted their horses, the white horse was nowhere to be seen.

The King sent for his own wizard.

"I paid twelve of my best elephants for that horse," he said. "You MUST find it."

The King's wizard was no fool. He knew a thing or two himself. 'Set a horse to catch a horse,' he thought, and changed himself into a black stallion.

The white horse was grazing in a field. He heard the black stallion galloping towards him, and changed himself into a large white eagle. He soared up into the sky on strong white wings.

The King's wizard, who certainly did know a thing or two, changed into a black eagle. He soared up into the sky on strong black wings.

The white eagle saw him coming and changed into a white hawk. The black eagle changed into a black kite and chased the hawk into the trees, where Bertram's brothers were sitting playing checkers.

The white hawk changed into a white checker piece and hid amongst the other pieces on the board.

The black kite changed into the King's wizard.

"May I have my checker piece?" he asked.

"These are OUR checker pieces," said Bertram's brothers.

"Count them. You will find you have one too many," said the King's wizard. Of course, when Bertram's brothers counted the pieces, they found they did have one too many.

But as the wizard put out his hand to pick it up, it changed into a scorpion with a sting in its tail. Whereupon the King's wizard turned into a snake. At which the scorpion changed into an even larger snake.

It was quite obvious that neither wizard was going to win the contest, so they changed themselves back into their own shapes and sat down to talk things over.

"Does the King feel cheated out of his elephants?" asked Bertram.

"He does," said the King's wizard. "And not without cause."

"I was only having fun," said Bertram. "I'll send them back at once."

"I'd go home myself, if only I knew the way," said the King's wizard, who sometimes, it would seem, did NOT know a thing or two.

"I'll take you," said Bertram. The two wizards changed themselves into black crows and flew off towards the palace.

Bertram's brothers said they much preferred their own way of having fun. All that changing from one thing to another was far too exhausting.

SNOW-WHITE AND ROSE-RED

Once there was a woman who lived in a lonely cottage in the middle of a wood. She had two daughters, one called Snow-White, and the other Rose-Red. One winter evening, when they were all sitting by the fire, there was a knock at the door.

"Someone must be seeking shelter from the cold," said the woman and went to open the door.

Standing on the doorstep, his black fur sprinkled with snow, was an enormous bear. Snow-White and Rose-Red took one look at his bright shining eyes, and his powerful claws, and ran to hide.

"You look very cold," said the woman to the bear. "Please come in and warm yourself by the fire."

"Do not be afraid," said the bear when he saw the children peeping at him. "I will not harm you."

"Will you help me brush the snow from my fur?" asked the bear, as the children crept nervously from their hiding place. They picked up the broom so that they could brush him without getting too close, but the bear was so friendly and it was such fun brushing a bear with a broom they soon forgot to be afraid.

The bear came to the house and slept by the fire every night throughout the long winter. He and the children became firm friends, and no matter how roughly the children played, the bear was always very gentle.

Then one day, as summer grew near, the bear said goodbye.

"I must go and protect my treasure from the dwarfs," he said. "They stay underground in winter but in summer they are everywhere. I fear they are not to be trusted."

One day, later that summer, when Snow-White and Rose-Red were in the middle of the woods picking wild strawberries, they saw a dwarf themselves. He was jumping up and down in a terrible rage. The end of his beard had caught in a crack in a fallen log and he couldn't get it out.

"How did it happen?" asked Snow-White, as she and Rose-Red did their best to pull him free.

"Not that it's any business of yours," grumbled the dwarf, "but I was driving a wedge into the crack to keep it open. The wedge popped out and the crack closed up again over my beard . . . Ouch! Ouch! You're hurting me! Be careful!"

"We can't get you out on our own," said Rose-Red. "I'll go and get some help."

"I can't wait that long . . . think of something yourself," grumbled the dwarf. And so Snow-White, thinking the dwarf would be pleased, took the scissors, which she always carried in her pocket, and cut through his beard. He was free, but the tip of his beard was growing out of the log like a fuzzy white fungus. The dwarf wasn't at all pleased. He picked up the sack of gold which was lying beside the log, and stomped off, without even the hint of a thank you.

A few days later, Snow-White and Rose-Red went to the river to catch fish. Who should they see there but the very same dwarf. He was in terrible trouble. The end of his beard had caught in his fishing line, and a fish was pulling the line, and him, into the river.

"Help me! Help me!" shrieked the dwarf, holding as tightly as he could to a bunch of reeds. He was slipping all the time.

"We must do something quickly or he will drown," said Rose-Red.

Snow-White took out her scissors and snipped the end off the dwarf's beard. The dwarf fell backwards into the reeds and the fish swam away. Was the dwarf grateful? Not at all! He picked up a sack of pearls which was lying in the reeds and stomped off with a bad-tempered glare and not even a hint of a thank you.

Some time later, Snow-White and Rose-Red were crossing the field when an eagle, which had been hovering over a rock, suddenly swooped low. There was a terrible cry. They ran to see what had happened. The eagle had its talons in the dwarf's coat and was lifting him from the ground.

"Help me!" shrieked the dwarf. Snow-White and Rose-Red caught hold of his legs and pulled . . . downwards. The eagle held on tight with his talons and pulled . . . upwards.

"You'll tear me in two!" shrieked the dwarf. But all that was torn was his coat, as the eagle continued to soar upwards and HE fell with a thud to the ground. Was he grateful at being rescued? No, he wasn't. "You should have been more careful, then you wouldn't have torn my coat," he grumbled. He picked up a sack of precious stones which was lying beside the rock and disappeared into a cave. Snow-White and Rose-Red were quite used to the dwarf's grumpy ways by now. They didn't expect a thank you. Which was just as well, because they didn't get one.

Later in the afternoon they caught the dwarf by surprise. He had emptied the sack of precious stones onto the ground and was gloating over their colors and their sparkle. He stamped his feet and shook his fists when he saw them. He was VERY annoyed.

"How DARE you spy on me!" he shouted. In the very middle of his rage an enormous black bear came ambling along the path.

The dwarf turned as pale as an uncooked pancake, and ran towards his cave. But the bear was quicker than he was and stood in his way.

"Don't eat me . . . please don't eat me!" The dwarf was shivering with fright. "You can have ALL my treasure! I'm too small and thin to eat! Eat those two wicked girls!"

The bear raised his paw and knocked the dwarf to the ground. Snow-White and Rose-Red were very frightened, but the bear called to them not to be afraid and they recognised his voice. As they ran to him, his bearskin fell to the ground. He wasn't a bear at all, but a king who had been bewitched by the dwarf, and the treasure the dwarf had been gloating over was his. Now the bad-tempered dwarf was dead, and the spell was broken.

MOTHER HOLLY

Once there were two step-sisters, who were as different as chalk and cheese. Martha was idle and never did a thing unless she HAD to, which wasn't very often for she was her mother's favorite. Anna was always busy. She HAD to be, for she was only a step-daughter.

One day, Anna was sitting in the garden spinning when she pricked her finger. A speck of blood fell onto the shuttle. She was trying to wash it clean when it slipped from her fingers and fell to the bottom of the well.

"YOU dropped it! YOU must go down and get it!" shouted her step-mother in such a rage that Anna had no choice but to do as she was told. She must have bumped her head as she fell, for she remembered nothing until she woke, and found herself in a pleasant field. She got to her feet and began to walk. Presently she came to an oven.

"Take me out . . . before I burn," creid the bread in the oven.

Anna took the bread from the oven and set it to cool.

A little further on she came to a tree.

"Shake me!" cried the tree. "My apples are ripe!"

Anna shook the tree. When all the apples had fallen she piled them veatly, then went on her way until she came to the house of a witch.

"You must come and work for me," said the witch. "Your most important task will be to shake my feather bed every morning. I am Mother Holly. If my bed is not shaken properly there will be no snow."

Mother Holly was very kind to Anna and for a while Anna was happy, but then she began to feel homesick.

"You have worked very hard," said Mother Holly, "and I will show you the way home." She took Anna to a hidden door. "Go through," said Mother Holly, handing her the lost shuttle. As Anna stepped through the door a shower of golden rain fell all about her and clung to her hair and her clothes.

"The gold is yours," said Mother Holly. "Goodbye my dear."

The next moment Anna found herself at home. As she ran across the yard, a rooster sitting on the fence crowed

"Cock a doodle do!

A golden girl is come to you!"

"Where have you been you bad girl!" shouted her step-mother running to the door. But when she saw the gold she quickly changed her tune. "Where did you get it? How did you get it?"

Anna told her everything that had happened.

"Martha shall have gold too," said her step-mother. "Go, sit by the well Martha, and spin. Do everything as Anna did."

Martha did not like spinning and she was in a hurry to get rich. She pricked her finger on a thorn to make it bleed. She squeezed her finger so that blood fell onto the shuttle, then she threw the shuttle into the well and jumped in after it.

Everything happened as before until Martha reached the oven.

"Take me out . . . before I burn!" cried the bread.

"And get my hands dirty! Certainly not!" snapped Martha.

"Shake me . . . my apples are ripe!" called the tree.

"What! And have one fall on my head! Certainly not!" snapped Martha, and hurried on to the witch's cottage.

"I will come and work for you," she said to Mother Holly, without waiting to be asked.

On the first day she worked well. On the second day she swept the dust under the hearth-rug and didn't bother to shake Mother Holly's mattress at all. On the third day she stayed in bed until mid-afternoon.

"It is time for you to go home," said Mother Holly.

"You must pay me first," said Martha greedily.

"Certainly, I will pay you," said Mother Holly, and led her to the hidden door. This time, instead of a shower of gold descending like rain, a shower of black pitch came pouring down. It covered Martha from head to foot. It was horrid!

"That is just payment for the work you have done," said Mother Holly sternly, and closed the door behind her.

When Martha ran sobbing across the yard to the house, the rooster sitting on the fence crowed,

"Cock a doodle do!
A dirty girl is come to you!"